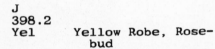

Tonweya and the Eagles

Tonweya and the Eagles

AND OTHER LAKOTA TALES

retold by ROSEBUD YELLOW ROBE

pictures by JERRY PINKNEY

Dial Books for Young Readers New York

Published by
Dial Books for Young Readers
A Division of Penguin Books USA Inc.
375 Hudson Street
New York, New York 10014

Second Edition
1 2 3 4 5 6 7 8 9 10
Design by Atha Tehon

Library of Congress Cataloging in Publication Data
Yellow Robe, Rosebud.
Tonweya and the eagles, and other Lakota tales.
Summary: A collection of animal tales first told by the Plains Indians,
interwoven with factual information about the Lakota people.
1. Teton Indians—Legends. 2. Indians of North America—Great
Plains—Legends. [1. Teton Indians—Legends. 2. Indians of North
America—Great Plains—Legends] I. Pinkney, Jerry. II. Title
E99.T34Y44   398.2   78-72470
ISBN 0-8037-8973-4
ISBN 0-8037-8974-2 lib. bdg.

Several of the stories in this book won awards at the
American Indian Art Exhibit in Scottsdale, Arizona.

In loving memory of

MY FATHER AND MOTHER

Contents

FOREWORD   *11*

Chano   *21*

The Lodge of the Bear   *24*

Chano's First Buffalo Hunt   *31*

The White Fox   *42*

Wastewin and the Beaver   *52*

The Boy Who Wore Turtle Shell Moccasins   *59*

The Wicked Sister-in-Law   *66*

Iktomi and the Red-Eyed Ducks   *86*

The Lakota Woman   *94*

Tonweya and the Eagles   *102*

EPILOGUE   *115*

GLOSSARY AND PRONUNCIATION GUIDE   *117*

Foreword

The stories in this book were told to me by my father, Canowicakte. Canowicakte was the boy Chano. Chano was a shortened name used for him. The *c* is pronounced like a *ch*, and the *a* as in *ah*.

My father was born in the southern part of what is now

Montana. He lived with his people, the Lakota-oyate, or Sioux nation, roaming the Plains of what are now South Dakota, North Dakota, Nebraska, Wyoming, and Montana. My grandfather was named Tasinagi, or Yellow Robe. He was the son of a hereditary chief. He had won his title to chieftainship as a fearless warrior and great hunter. He too was a leader of his people. My grandmother was named Tahcawin, meaning fawn or female deer. My father was her favorite child because he was her firstborn.

When my father was an infant, my grandfather Tasinagi and my grandmother Tahcawin gave a huge feast for the great men of the tribe in his honor. At that time he was named Canowicakte, meaning kill-in-the-woods. The lobes of both his ears were pierced so that he might wear earrings. Tasinagi gave away two of his best ponies.

Canowicakte spent many hours in the tipi of his grandfather and grandmother. They were his tutors in legends and history of the tribe. He was expected to memorize all these stories so that he in turn would be able to relate them to his children. He was taught respect and reverence for Wakan-tanka, the Great Mystery. He learned of the great and inspiring deeds of the famous chiefs, warriors, and medicine men. He was trained in the old customs of how to make bows and arrows for hunting and for wars. He learned to ride ponies bareback. He learned how to hunt deer and buffalo. He enjoyed wrestling, swimming, and footracing with his companions.

Often Canowicakte followed his father on his hunting trips and learned how to kill a deer or elk and drag it back to camp over the prairie.

Living so close to nature he became familiar with the characteristics and habits of the animals and birds. He knew that his people did not kill buffalo or other game for pleasure. They killed only for use.

He saw his first white man when his parents made camp near one of the trading posts along the Missouri River. He was playing near the camp with his brother when he saw a creature coming toward them. It had long fair hair and a beard and was wearing a large hat and a fringed buckskin suit. It carried a musket on its shoulder. Chano couldn't decide if it was a man or an animal of some kind. As the creature came near the boys, Chano decided it was an evil spirit. For the first time in his life his bravery failed him. He screamed, and leaving his brother behind, he ran to his father in the tipi. His father laughed when he heard the story of the evil spirit. He told Chano he had seen a white man. He told the boys not to go very far away or the white man would kidnap them.

Chano remembered warriors coming back and telling exciting tales of their battles with the white men who promised to stay away from the Lakota-oyate lands but who were always forgetting their promises.

When Chano was about fifteen years old, his dreams of glory in an Indian world vanished. General R. H. Pratt came to the headmen of the tribe and asked them to send one of their children east to a school called Carlisle. He told them that life would change rapidly for them. The buffalo were being killed off and reservations were being formed. He explained that the leaders should know about the new world so different from the Indian way of living.

Against his will my father was given to General Pratt to go away to Carlisle. I have pictures of my father taken when he first arrived at the school with skin clothing, moccasins, and long hair. Then pictures when his clothing had been taken away and he was given the uniform of the school to wear. His hair was cut short. For a long time he thought his mother had died. He had been the first taken to the barber to have his hair cut. Among the Sioux it is a sign of mourning to do so. He thought the other boys were mourning her too, as they had their hair cut.

The children were not allowed to speak their own language, only English, and many weeks had passed by before my father learned that his mother was still alive.

The teachers were very kind to him, but until he learned the language and understood them, he did not trust them. He was a good student. He took part in all the athletics and played on the football team. During the summers he worked on the farms. He also attended the Moody Institute summer school at Northfield, Massachusetts.

Before he left Carlisle, Chauncey Yellow Robe, which was now Canowicakte's name, was chosen to represent the North American Indians at the Congress of Nations at the opening of the World's Columbian Exposition in Chicago.

Canowicakte graduated with honors with the class of 1895. Shortly thereafter he entered government service and spent the greater part of his life at various Indian schools. He was for many years at the large nonreservation boarding school at Rapid City, South Dakota.

At Rapid City my father met my mother. They fell in love and were married and continued living and working there. My father was disappointed that he did not have a son but soon reconciled himself to his three daughters.

We were very lucky to have parents who taught us about our cultural background and who tried as the Lakotas had for generations to tell us the stories they had heard in their youth. After they were dead, I found several of the stories written out in my mother's and father's handwriting.

My father became very well known for his activities, first with The Society of American Indians. He was much sought after by many organizations as a speaker and soon became known as a "bridge between two cultures."

He spoke out many times critically, and in such a way that he was considered a spokesman for the Sioux.

My father presided at the ceremonies at Deadwood, South Dakota, when the Sioux inducted President Calvin Coolidge into the tribe.

Despite his distaste for the way in which the American Indian was depicted in movies he was persuaded to play a leading role in *The Silent Enemy*, written and produced by Douglas Burden, a trustee of the American Museum of Natural History. This was the first movie produced with an all-Indian cast and no professional actors. It was the story of the Ojibways' struggle against their silent enemy, hunger.

During this time he was also running for Congress in his home state of South Dakota.

He did the talking prologue for the picture *The Silent Enemy*; since the prologue was made in New York City studios, it was last to be filmed. During that time he caught a cold that became pneumonia. He died at the Rockefeller Institute Hospital after a brief illness.

Shortly after my father's death President Coolidge, usually a man of few words, wrote a wonderful tribute to him. In part he said, "He represented a trained and intelligent contact between two different races. He was a born leader who realized that the destiny of the Indian is indissolubly bound up with the destiny of our country. His loyalty to his tribe and his people made him a most patriotic American."

Tonweya and the Eagles

Chano

Chano was born in a skin tipi during a blizzard somewhere along the Rosebud River in what is now southern Montana.

Tasinagi, Chano's father, following an old custom went out into the curtain of snow blowing angrily around the tipis and called, "Waziya, your wife has fallen over a cliff and is hurt." Waziya, the god of the Storm, was supposed to be so worried about his wife that he would return swiftly to the Northland to help her.

When Chano was older and had experienced several severe blizzards, he decided that Waziya did not love his wife very much because that time and many other times he stayed around for several days before going home.

A few weeks after his birth his mother, Tahcawin, made a keya, or small turtle of deerskin. She stuffed the turtle with down and the dried navel cord belonging to Chano. Tahcawin sewed two strings on the underside of the turtle. She believed that if Chano wore the keya tied to his belt he was bound to her as much after birth as before. Chano was very careful not to lose the keya. He loved his mother very much and knew as long as he had his good-luck piece with him, no harm could come to him.

As Chano grew older, his grandparents were chosen by his parents to be his teachers in the history of the tribe and the old customs. His uncle Iron Plume and his father were his tutors in the way to hunt, ride, swim, and run.

He had heard of the strange white men who came from the East and wanted the lands of the Lakotas. He saw warriors who came back victorious over the white enemy. He heard many discussions by the men of the tribe about something called Treaties that were to be signed. Some of his relatives were against the Treaties; they did not understand them and they could not read. Chano's father had signed one in 1868. Later when Chano was a young man, Tasinagi told him he had not signed another one that the white men claimed had his mark on it.

Chano loved his Lakota life: the changing seasons, the travels with the tribe from one camping place to another, the hours spent learning, preparing to be a man.

When he grew up, he cherished wonderful memories of events like his first buffalo hunt, his first glimpse of the red-winged eagles of Tonweya. He remembered too the countless evenings around the fire when his father told age-old and well-loved stories, some frightening, some sad, some funny.

In his boyhood and throughout his life Chano heard and learned by heart many, many stories. Those that follow are a few of his special favorites.

The Lodge of the Bear

It was the Month of Changing Colors. The days were warm and bright.

Chano was excited. His parents had decided to visit the parents of his mother, Tahcawin. He had heard them talking well into the night about the trip. He thought perhaps this time he might go along. His mother's people were the Hunk-papa and were then camping along the Powder River in Montana. Perhaps he would see his mother's nephew Sitting Bull. He had heard many wonderful stories about him.

The next day it was decided to take Chano along on the dangerous journey. It was a long trip around the Black Hills, the Paha-sapa. They must return before winter set in, so they would have to travel fast.

Chano packed his belongings in a rawhide container called a parfleche, said good-bye to all his friends, and looked after his pony.

His mother and father were busy all that day packing parfleche cases of food and clothing and planning their way of travel.

Early the next morning Chano ran down to the river, splashed in the cool clear water, and then returned to join his parents for their first meal of the day.

Long before dawn they were many miles away from camp. When the ball of fire appeared over the horizon, they could no longer see the tipis.

The ponies kept on at a loping trot, fast enough to cover many miles, but slow enough for the riders to enjoy the beauty around them. They passed several prairie dog villages and all three laughed at the sight of the prairie dogs sitting up near their homes, looking just like little old men.

Tasinagi told Chano how these little animals made their homes in deep burrows or caves; often owls shared the homes of the prairie dogs.

The ponies were very careful not to step in the holes the prairie dogs made. Once Chano's pony shied suddenly. Right in his path was a big coiled rattlesnake. Chano patted his pony's neck, and the snake, seeing no one was going to harm him, uncoiled and glided away.

Suddenly in the late afternoon Chano saw a most peculiar sight. It was a solitary mountain rising abruptly out of the plains. Actually it was a butte, not a mountain, for it was almost a perfect circle and the top was as flat as the plain. Its sides were straight up and down, and as they drew nearer Chano noticed long black lines that ran from the top down to the bottom. At closer range these lines turned out to be deep furrows that looked like deep scratches in the butte's side. It was so odd, Chano asked his father what it was.

"That," said Tasinagi, "is Mato Tipi. The Bear's Lodge. Perhaps your mother will tell you about it."

Tahcawin motioned to Chano to ride beside her if he

wanted to hear the story. Chano rode over beside his mother and listened.

"Long ago a band of Lakotas camped near the Black Hills, the Paha-sapa. Among them were a young boy and his sister, children of one of the wise men of the band. One day the boy and girl went out to pick berries. They wandered on and on, never realizing how far they were from home.

"Suddenly they heard a deep growl behind them. Turning, they saw a huge bear and to their dismay they also saw that not a tipi was in sight. They were all alone on the prairie.

"As they had no weapons, they decided that the only thing for them to do was run. When the bear saw them run, he started after them, growling more fiercely than before.

"The poor children, terrified, ran as they had never run before, but despite all their efforts the bear gained on them steadily. Realizing there was no escape, they stopped and turned toward their pursuer. If they were to die, then they would die like brave warriors, facing their enemy.

"When the bear saw them stop, he too stopped. Standing up on his hind legs he glowered at them.

"While they stood like that, the little girl said to her brother: 'Brother, let us call upon Wakan-tanka, the Great Mystery. Surely He will help us.' So the two of them, still facing the big bear, raised their arms to the sky and called to Wakan-tanka to help them.

"A strange thing happened. The ground on which they stood began to rise, and by the time the astonished bear decided to charge, the two children were safe on top of a tall butte.

"The bear was so angry, he tried again and again to climb the steep sides of the place where the children had found refuge. He would back away, then running swiftly, he would jump up and try to reach the mountaintop. But each time he missed and as he went sliding back to the bottom, his big sharp claws made the scratches you see running up and down the sides. He persevered until he had clawed his way completely around the sides and then he stopped because he was exhausted. In fact he was so tired that he couldn't move and he died of starvation and thirst at the foot of the butte.

"The boy and girl lived all their lives on the butte and after they died, their spirits were often seen by people passing that way. Some might think it is only a few fleecy white

clouds, but wise ones know it is the children playing and dancing. In the summer when the thunder rolls, people say it is Bear growling."

By the time Chano's mother had finished the story, they were quite close to the mountain. It was growing late and Tasinagi decided to camp at its base. Several times that night Chano awoke. He was sure he heard the Bear growling. Once he looked up and by the light of the stars he saw two little clouds high above him. He knew it was the spirits of the two children and he knew they would watch over him, so he went back to sleep.

Chano's First Buffalo Hunt

Chano was disappointed. Tahcawin and Tasinagi had decided to turn back to the Belle Fourche and Iron Plume's camp. There had been too many signs of the Crow and it would be best for Chano to stay with his uncle Iron Plume; they could travel faster and more safely without him.

It was a good day's travel to Iron Plume's camp. Chano was delighted to see the tipis and smell the odor of buffalo ribs cooking.

Chano was happy to stay with Uncle Iron Plume. Iron Plume had given him the pony he was riding. He always had an interesting life in the Iron Plume camp. Chano said good-bye to his parents a few days later and then began to help his uncle.

Iron Plume was very busy. The Month of Falling Leaves would soon be coming, and then the Month of Falling Snow and Cracking Trees. Before that time a supply of meat and berries must be put away. They had dried much meat during the summer but they would need even more.

Hunting parties went out every day and returned loaded with game. Chano helped his aunt dry the meat in strips and then make wasna. The dried meat was ground up with fat and wild cherries and then stored away in cakelike shapes for use during travel and the winter months.

The camp was so busy hunting that Iron Plume asked Chano to look after his horses. This was quite an honor, for in those days one's wealth was judged by the number of horses one owned. Iron Plume had many horses and Chano loved to ride lazily about with the grazing herd on those beautiful autumn days. The leaves of the trees and plants were all colors now when the sun showed through them. Sometimes Chano threw himself down on the ground and then it seemed as if mother earth sent wave after wave of strength through his body. He was happy here all alone. It was so quiet and peaceful. Very often strange small animal brothers came close to him and made friends. He learned much of the habits of all these animal friends.

Iron Plume had shown him how to make his own bows and arrows. Sometimes he worked at this while watching the horses. He made several bows of cherry, wild plum, and crab apple wood; then he finally succeeded in making a really fine bow for buffalo hunting. He learned that the length of the arrow depended on the length of his arm. He also learned one of the many lessons of economy. Iron Plume told him that wise hunters picked a light, flexible wood for the shaft of their arrows so that if the animal fell on the arrow, it would bend, not break. Then the arrow could be used again. Chano experimented until he found that Juneberry and currant shafts rarely broke.

Chano found that he must learn a lot about arrows beside getting the right wood. It was very important to feather one end of the arrow properly so it would fly true to its mark. He scratched long zigzag lines on the shaft. This represented the lightning and was to make the arrow fly as fast as the lightning itself. All his arrows had his own secret mark so that if anyone else should claim the animal he shot, he could prove by his arrows it was his. He marked his arrows with the earth-color red because mother earth had always befriended him during the long days when he was alone with her.

Iron Plume also explained to him that in nocking his arrows for hunting he must see that the nock–the sort of notch at the end of the arrow shaft into which the bowstring fits–allowed the arrowhead to lie vertically. The ribs of an animal were vertical and it would be easy for the arrowhead to slip in between them. The arrowhead was to be firmly tied on so it would slip out easily when pulled. Also he must so nock his shaft that the arrow points used in battle lay flat, for the ribs of man lay flat also, just the opposite of the ribs of animals.

Chano learned how to make arrow points. The hunting arrows were different from those for war. Hunting points were long and roughly triangular and fastened securely to the shaft. One could pull them out without too much trouble. The war points were deeply barbed and fastened lightly to the shaft. The deep barbs ripped at the wound when one tried to pull them out and usually only the shaft came away, while the point remained in the body.

The bow and arrow Chano realized were very important. To secure food and defend oneself from the enemy they had to be made with great skill.

Iron Plume took Chano on a few small-game hunts and Chano proved himself a good hunter. But Iron Plume said Chano was still too young for a buffalo hunt and should wait until he had more experience.

One day when his uncle was away visiting a neighboring camp, a runner brought word that a large herd of buffalo was grazing just a few miles away.

Immediately the whole camp was astir. Men made ready for the hunt. Chano noticed some of the older boys were going along this time. It was late in the season and there would not be many more hunting trips. He decided he was as big as some of the boys and he could shoot better than they could. He had practiced riding his pony, controlling him with his legs, and shooting targets with his arrows. His pony was an excellent buffalo runner.

In an instant Chano made up his mind. He picked up his bow and a quiver of arrows, threw a piece of rope around his pony's neck, jumped on his back, and was off to join the other hunters.

Chano felt excited and strong as he rode with the men. Two or three miles from camp they saw hundreds of animals. To Chano it looked like a huge herd. There were cows, big bulls, and some calves in the herd, and several of the buffalo were out in all directions acting as scouts to warn when danger was near.

The hunters circled the herd until they were downwind from them, and keeping behind high ground, managed to get within a few hundred feet before they were discovered. The old buffalo scouts raised their heads to give the alarm, and with a huge bellow of surprise and fear the whole herd wheeled and stampeded away from the hunters. The hunting ponies of the Lakota managed soon to overtake the fleeing animals.

For a moment Chano was stunned by the thunderous roar made by the hundreds of pounding hooves and the big cloud of dust that was raised. Before Chano realized it, his pony had worked himself right into the herd. Buffalo rubbed against his legs on each side. Their great bodies pressed around him and he could feel their heat. Once in a while one of them would let out a snort of fear and Chano could feel the gust of hot breath against his body.

Chano did not know if he was on the edge of the herd or right in the middle. Dust was everywhere. He could see only the animals near him.

Chano was a little frightened at first. He knew if his pony tripped or if he should fall off his back, he would be trampled to death.

He took heart as he noticed his pony was enjoying the hunt. The pony flattened down his ears and with a snort of delight raced along with the herd.

Chano, riding skillfully, carefully fitted an arrow to his bow and shot at the nearest buffalo. It was an old bull and the arrow hit him near his shoulder in the heavy mane. It did not stop him. Chano realized too late that he had wasted one of his precious arrows. He planned what to do next; he was enjoying himself now as much as his pony was.

He waited until he came abreast of a fine yearling cow on his left. Fitting an arrow to his bow he took careful aim and let it go. It struck her right behind the shoulder and while she did not fall, she slowed down and staggered along. He shot a second arrow and this time she dropped. To Chano's relief he noticed he was at the edge of the herd by now and by skillfully guiding his horse he managed to drop out of the hunt.

He turned his pony back. He could see the cow he had

shot. When he came up to her, she was dead. He looked down at her, his first buffalo, killed with the bow and arrow he had made with his own hands. His heart sang. He raised his hands to the sky and gave thanks to Wakan-tanka.

When he dismounted, he took his hunting knife and began to skin the buffalo the way he had seen his father and uncle do it. It was no easy task for a boy, but he kept at it until he was done. He cut the choicest portions of the meat and tied it up in a piece of the fresh skin. The heart, liver, and kidneys he wrapped separately. They were a special present for his aunt and uncle.

When Chano tried to tie the fresh meat onto his pony, the frightened pony reared and backed off. Chano coaxed the pony to him and rubbed some of the fresh blood over the pony's nose. When the pony discovered that the scent of blood did no harm to him, he was submissive and allowed Chano to tie the bundles of meat on his back.

On his ride back to camp Chano sang his first brave song. He was happy that he had not been afraid, that he had killed his first buffalo, that he too could join with the other men of the tribe in hunting.

Chano reached camp long after the others had returned. He hurried to unload his horse; he watered him and then turned him loose to graze with the other ponies. He washed himself and then entered the tipi. He sat down against his backrest and looked at the evening meal, roast buffalo ribs. He ate heartily.

After they had all eaten, Chano's uncle looked at him and said, "Chano, do you not know that it was wrong to disobey me and join the hunters today? Both your aunt and I were worried. What if you had had an accident? What could we tell your parents?"

"I am very sorry, Uncle," Chano replied. "But I—well—when I saw all the others going, I was so excited I just went along."

"I understand, my son," said Iron Plume. "I was a boy a long time ago and I forgot at times too."

Then he asked Chano about the hunt. Chano replied that everyone got at least one buffalo and some two or three.

"Did you get one?" asked his uncle with a smile.

For answer Chano went outside and dragged in the big bundles of meat. His aunt and uncle were pleased with his modesty and even more pleased with the delicacies he had brought back for them.

Iron Plume immediately sent a crier through the camp to tell everyone of Chano's success on his first buffalo hunt. He also invited them to a feast in Chano's honor the next day.

It is an old custom to give a feast in honor of a great deed done by a loved one. It was a fine feast. Everyone ate, sang, and danced. Iron Plume gave away many horses in honor of the occasion. Many said how brave it was for such a young boy to bring down a buffalo all by himself. In his heart Chano sang his brave song again.

When the feast was over and they were alone again, Iron Plume called Chano to him and told him that Tasinagi would be coming to take him home sometime during the next few days.

Iron Plume said, "And I cannot return to him what he brought me."

"Why?" said Chano. "I'm here just the same."

"No, my son," replied Iron Plume, "Tasinagi brought me a boy and I return to him a mighty hunter." Then he smiled at Chano.

This time Chano sang his brave song not only in his heart but aloud so that his aunt and uncle could hear him. He was a man–no longer a boy.

The White Fox

It was late in the Month of Changing Colors, and Tasinagi
and Tahcawin decided it was time to go to the buffalo berry
thickets to gather berries before the frost.

Most of the Lakota women waited until the first frost;
then after placing blankets under the bushes, they beat the

berries off with long sticks. Tahcawin knew that Chano and Tasinagi liked the tart taste of the berries before the frost. She always made them their special buffalo berry jam, even though it was very difficult to pick the berries, for the bushes were covered with thorns. Tahcawin wrapped her arms with soft pieces of buckskin before she reached into the thorny bushes.

Chano helped as much as he could, but the thorns were just too much for him. He and his father watched Tahcawin admiringly. When she had filled a couple of pouches, they began the long ride back to camp.

As they rode, Chano begged his father for a story to help pass the time and without too much urging Tasinagi began:

"Know you, Chano, that Fox has always been called the animal trickster. And this story will show that he richly deserves this name. Years ago Fox the Trickster played so many tricks on the Lakota people that he almost drove them wild. He grew so bold that he would even raid the camp during the daytime. He would help himself to the meat that was drying or even cooking in the pot. As for jam or honey or wasna it was not safe to let them out of your sight even for a moment. Turn your back even for a short time and you would be lucky if they had not disappeared before you

43

turned around again. He even went so far as to stampede the horses. Finally he became such a general nuisance that the entire village tried to trap or shoot him. But Fox always escaped. Finally the chief sent out word that he would give a rich reward and high honors to whoever rid the camp of this troublemaker.

"Now there was in the camp at that time a young boy of ten summers who made up his mind to catch this wily old fox. This boy's name was Waditaka, which means brave, and he lived alone with his old grandmother. He knew that if he succeeded, he would not only get the reward and honors but would be looked upon as great and wise. One evening he said to his grandmother, 'Grandmother, have I your permission to catch the wicked fox?' 'Yes,' said Grandmother, 'but how can you do this when so many others much wiser than you have failed?' 'Because,' replied Waditaka, 'I have dreamed a dream. Three times have I dreamed the same thing. And each time the four winds came to me and promised me their help. They are my spirit friends and I feel sure that if I pay them a visit, they will show me how to catch the old fox.' Grandmother nodded gravely, for she knew the power of dreams. If the four winds had come to her Waditaka when he was asleep, then surely he would succeed where all others had failed.

"Slowly she arose and went to the rear of the tipi. When she returned to Waditaka, she had a parfleche in her arms. And when she opened it, there was the most beautiful blanket he had ever seen. It was made entirely of white rabbit skins. Never had he known she owned such a beautiful thing. 'My son,' said Grandmother, 'the four winds make their homes in far-off places. If you go to them on foot, it will take many days and the journey will be long and hard. Take this blanket. It is good medicine. Wrap it around you and it will instantly transport you to any place you desire. Here it is and may your journey be successful.'

"Waditaka thanked her and throwing the blanket over his shoulders he made the wish to be taken to the home of South Wind. Suddenly he found himself standing before her. South Wind was a beautiful maiden. Her touch was warm and gentle as she welcomed Waditaka. 'Well, my little friend, I see you've come. What can I do for you?' 'Oh, beautiful South Wind, help me catch the wicked fox. He is making so much trouble for my people,' said Waditaka. 'Did I not promise you in your dreams that I would help? Surely will I do that which you ask,' answered South Wind. 'But if I were you, I would ask the other winds to help also so that this wicked fox will not by any chance escape.'

"Waditaka told her he would do that very thing and wrapping his blanket about him he wished South Wind a polite good-bye. In a twinkling of the eye he was at the home of West Wind. West Wind was a strong young brave. His touch was cool and dry. It made the blood go tingling through your veins. But at the same time it made you very tired. He listened to Waditaka's story and immediately promised to aid him also. 'I think,' said Waditaka after he thanked West Wind, 'that I will see East Wind next.' And no sooner said than done. East Wind was a maiden also and, like her sister South Wind, very beautiful. But whereas South Wind was always smiling, East Wind had the habit of shedding bitter tears over the least little thing. She was smiling when Waditaka started telling her about the wicked fox, but as she listened, her beautiful eyes brimmed over with tears and before he was half through, she was weeping. Sadder and sadder she grew. And the sadder she grew, the more she wept. Waditaka could hardly finish his story, so busy was he trying to keep his blanket out of the puddles of water formed by East Wind's tears. Finally she managed to control herself a little, and though

her eyes were still streaming, she promised to help the
other winds get rid of old Fox. At the mere thought of the
wicked things he had done to Waditaka's people she began
to cry again. And by the time she had finished saying good-
bye to him, poor Waditaka was almost as wet as she was.

"He had one more visit to make. Far away in the land of
eternal snow and ice dwelt North Wind. He was a great
strong warrior who was ready to go on the warpath at the
least excuse. When he was aroused, he roared fiercely. His
touch was freezing cold and carried death and destruction
with it. He listened to Waditaka and immediately agreed
to help him. 'Ho, ho hey,' he thundered, 'go back to your
people and tell them they are no longer to be troubled by
Fox. I'll see to that.' Waditaka thanked him but made the
mistake of telling him that the other winds had agreed to
help also. When North Wind heard this, he let out a roar
and said that he did not need any help from the other
winds, he was perfectly capable of handling a little thing
like that alone. North Wind was very conceited. He worked
himself up into such a fury that Waditaka grabbed his
blanket and wrapping himself up made the wish to be back
home. And in less time than it would take you to say Canowicakte, there he was beside his grandmother. She was very

glad to see him back again. 'Grandmother,' he said, 'tomorrow our troubles will be over. Tomorrow the four winds are going to catch old Fox for me.'

"The next day the Fox started out on one of his usual forays. He intended this time to steal all the dried meat he could possibly find. He started toward the west. He had not gone far when West Wind began to blow on him. In a few moments he felt hot and tired and thirsty. Just then South Wind began to blow and that made him remember that there was a lovely spring of cold water in her direction. He started toward it and all the while South Wind blew gently, bringing him scents of faraway places. And it was not long before she lulled him to sleep. Then South Wind, calling her sister East Wind to do her part, went on her way.

"East Wind looked down at Fox for a moment. When she remembered what a bad trickster he really was, she began to weep, softly at first, and her gentle tears falling lightly on Fox only served to lull him into deeper slumber. But when East Wind began to cry in real earnest, he awoke. Of course he didn't know that it was East Wind weeping. To him it was just raining very hard, and as it was anything but pleasant, he started off to find shelter. But

East Wind followed him wherever he went and by now she was feeling very, very sad. Her tears streamed down in torrents and in a short time Fox was soaked to the skin. His beautiful bushy tail hung down in the mud all wet and bedraggled, and to make matters worse, he could not find even the smallest shelter where he could crawl in out of the rain.

"Suddenly off in the distance came a big growl. Another, nearer and louder. Poor East Wind stopped a moment in alarm. She knew what that noise was. It was terrible North Wind coming down their way. She was so frightened that she gave Fox one last look and blew away as fast as she could go. She much preferred not to meet North Wind while he was in a fighting mood.

"Down came the North Wind in a flurry of snow. He raved, he howled, he roared. And when he caught sight of Fox, he just about blew him to bits. 'So you're the wicked fox who has been causing all the trouble around here. I'll soon attend to you,' he bellowed. And suiting the action to the word, he began to blow his icy cold breath on poor Fox. And the trickster, wet and tired as he was, did not have the strength to move. North Wind blew harder and harder. Each breath was colder than the last and in no time at all

the water on Fox's coat froze and he found himself encased in a cover of silent, glistening ice.

"With a final terrible blow that made everyone for miles around huddle close to their fires North Wind picked up the ice-coated Fox and transported him far up into the Northland. There he placed Fox in the white snow and ice where Fox lives to this very day.

"When Fox was at last released from the block of ice, he moved over the frozen Northland hunting for food. He had been so frightened by his terrible experience that his fur coat had turned completely white. He blended into the landscape, which made it easier for him to stalk his prey. But he never again lived in such luxury and plenty as he had among the Lakota people."

Chano sighed. "Animals and people are never satisfied with their lives, are they?"

Tasinagi replied, "It is good to be ambitious, but always be thankful for all the good things Wakan-tanka gives us. And now, you see, here we are almost back at the camp."

Wastewin and the Beaver

Tahcawin was watching Chano play with his two bear cub pets. Her son rolled and wrestled with the two cubs and every once in a while it seemed that the two cubs had pinned him down on the ground. But Chano always had a defense. He would tickle them on their stomachs and they would collapse on their backs, four paws in the air, enjoying the sensation.

Both Chano and his mother laughed at the cubs and Chano called out to her, "Did you see them smile? Look, they are really smiling."

He stopped tickling them and went over to his mother. "Ina, Mother," he said, "I think that my cubs are the best pets to have. They are my best friends. They go everywhere with me. They even like to swim."

Tahcawin agreed with her son. But she replied, "Everyone has a special pet. Would you like to hear the story of a girl and her pet beaver?"

Chano begged, "Tell me about her please." He stroked the cubs on their backs until they settled down quietly.

Tahcawin said, "This is a long ago story. . . . Once there lived in one of the Lakota-oyate lands a very beautiful girl named Wastewin."

Chano interrupted, "That means good."

Tahcawin replied, "Yes, and Wastewin was as good as she was beautiful. Her father and mother were very proud of her but sad because their only child had no husband. The young men of the tribe had courted her, but she had accepted no one. One day a group of hunters from another land rode into the camp. They brought plenty of meat with them and that evening as all were feasting, Wastewin felt someone watching her. She looked at the man who was openly staring at her and to her amazement she felt that she knew him. He was handsome and strong. Speaking with some of the women, she discovered that his name was Wayuwaka, meaning Peacemaker. They told her that he was a great warrior and fine hunter and all the young women of his tribe wished he would choose them for his wife. They looked at her curiously because this was the first time she had shown an interest in any man.

"Wastewin rose and wandered away from the feast toward her tipi. By the time she reached it, the young man was standing before her.

"He said, 'Wastewin, we know each other. I have known you and long waited for you to come to me. Will you go away with me now and be my wife?'

"As he touched her hand, Wastewin was so overwhelmed with love, she said, 'Yes, I will come with you.' She feared her parents would be shocked that their daughter would go off with a strange man, someone she had just met. So she told him that she would pack her things and leave them out in back of the tipi. Later when all were asleep, she would meet him there. The signal that he was there was to be a cough.

"Now Wastewin had a pet beaver who followed her everywhere and that night she took Beaver to bed with her. When she heard her lover cough, she bundled Beaver under her blanket and crept out of the tipi. It was very dark that night. A man wrapped in a blanket was waiting behind the tipi and she followed him quickly and quietly away from the camp. They traveled until they came to a wide river. There they stood on the bank and Wastewin said to her companion, 'Beaver can swim the river but I am not a good swimmer.'

"The man beside her turned, and dropping his blanket, revealed that he was not Wayuwaka. This man was a creature all Lakota people feared. He was called Double Face because he had two faces, one where it was supposed to be and one on the back of his head. Thick and very long hair covered the scalp between the faces. Double Face had overheard the plans. He had waylaid Wayuwaka and tied him to a tree.

"Wastewin was so shocked when she saw Double Face that she could not even scream. She clutched Beaver to her and turned and tried to run away. Double Face reached out and caught her quickly. He commanded her to lie on his back as he swam across the river and he threw her pet into the water.

"The girl clung to Double Face, so frightened she did not notice that Beaver was swimming right along beside them. When they reached the other side, Beaver quietly followed them.

"Double Face walked with the girl until they came to a big tipi in the woods. No one else lived nearby. He took the girl into the tipi and after he ate, he stretched out on the ground and placed his head on her lap. He told her he was tired and wanted to rest. He commanded her to comb his hair as it would help him to fall asleep.

"Wastewin obeyed. The porcupine quill hairbrush did not work well on Double Face's long hair, so with her fingers she began combing his hair and rubbing his forehead. He quickly fell asleep. When she was sure he was sound asleep, she took a long strand of his hair and tied it with a double knot to one of the tipi poles. She repeated this with another strand of hair until his hair spread out like a giant spider web in the tipi. She eased his head onto a piece of fur she rolled up and then she crawled out under the hair. Outside Beaver was waiting for her. She picked him up and ran for the river. She ran along it to a point where it became narrow and then Beaver quickly cut down trees with his strong teeth and made a bridge across. Wastewin and Beaver just reached the other side when

they heard Double Face racing along the shore. Beaver immediately began gnawing at the wooden bridge. Double Face started to run across the bridge, but just as he reached the center it collapsed, pinning him down in the water.

"Wastewin and Beaver hurried to the village. There everyone welcomed them with much rejoicing, for they had feared they had been taken away forever.

"Wayuwaka had confessed his plan to Wastewin's father and mother when he was found the next day. He had been very upset that he could not rescue his loved one.

"The father and mother had already accepted Wayuwaka as their son and relied on him for comfort in their distress. Now they all were together as they should be and everyone was happy.

"That evening there was a great feast and dancing. Beaver was a celebrated guest and his bravery was recited in song and story."

Chano sighed. "Beaver was a great friend to Wastewin and I wonder what happened to Double Face?"

Tahcawin said sadly, "I'm afraid Double Face escaped. As you know, we still have many stories about the evil one. Let us hope none of us ever sees Double Face."

Chano agreed wholeheartedly.

The Boy Who Wore
Turtle Shell Moccasins

Chano watched his father part his mother's long black hair from the center of her forehead across the top of the head and down to the nape of her neck. Then carefully Tasinagi began to brush Tahcawin's hair with a porcupine quill hairbrush. Chano felt close to both his parents and very proud of them. He knew that only men who loved their wives very much combed and braided their wives' hair. His father was singing a little song just for his mother as he painted the part of her hair with red paint. Tahcawin looked beautiful with her hair newly braided.

"I'm very lucky to have you both," said Chano.

Tasinagi laughed and replied, "And we're lucky to have you, my son. May I tell you a story about a boy who discovered one must always treasure lucky things and people?"

"Hakela, Last Born, was the youngest of four brothers. Because he was so young, he was very often left at home with his grandmother. His brothers loved him, but he was still too little to go on hunting trips with them. His grandmother realized how much he missed his brothers when they were away so she made him a gift, a strange pair of moccasins fashioned from turtle shells. When Hakela put them on, he could run like the wind. Every step he took was like two big steps. Everyone loved to watch Turtle Moccasin Boy run. Even his brothers envied him his turtle shell moccasins. But Grandmother had already given each of the brothers a gift that was particularly lucky for him.

"For the oldest brother Grandmother made a beautiful coup stick. She expected him to become a great warrior among the Lakota people. It was considered the greatest honor to touch the live enemy, to 'count coup.' The coup stick was beautifully ornamented and First Brother carried it proudly at all the ceremonies.

"Second Brother was given a beautiful quiver of arrows. It was so unusually made that Second Brother used it only when going on the warpath. There was one arrow among the others he considered particularly lucky. He used a different set for hunting because the arrows for hunting were securely fastened to the shaft and could be used again.

"For Third Brother Grandmother made a beautiful porcupine quill strike-a-light bag that contained flints and tinder for starting a fire. Third Brother need never eat uncooked food nor fear for the cold and he would always have fire to protect him from animals at night.

"Hakela, Last Born, had been forbidden to use any of the gifts Grandmother had made for his brothers. He had promised never to touch them.

"Early one morning the three older brothers went off on a hunting expedition. Hakela stayed in the tipi. He was disappointed he could not go along. Suddenly he saw a beautiful red bird fly in the door and circle and dart around the tipi. It was so lovely that Hakela wished to catch it for his brothers. He decided to shoot the scarlet bird and offer the beautiful feathers to them. He tried to shoot it with his own bow and arrows but missed as it circled over him in great distress. At last he grabbed his older brother's lucky arrow and succeeded in shooting the bird which flew out the door with the arrow sticking out of its side.

"Hakela, feeling he needed all the magical luck of his brothers' belongings, hastily seized the coup stick and the strike-a-light bag. He put on his turtle shell moccasins and followed the scarlet one. He knew he had to rescue his brother's lucky arrow and he hoped he would be able to extract it. Even though Hakela was frightened, he followed the bird as closely and as fast as he could. When he came to a distant camp, he asked the people if they had seen a red bird flying with an arrow piercing its body. They replied, 'We have not seen a red bird, but Red Plume just raced by with an arrow piercing his side.'

"Hakela was dismayed to find that the red bird had turned into a man, Red Plume. Such mystery bewildered him. He asked what direction the man had taken. They replied that they believed he had gone toward the camp beyond the next one. Hakela with his turtle moccasins ran past the next camp without stopping. Just outside the second camp he saw an old man carrying a bundle on his back. 'Grandfather, where are you going?' asked Hakela.

"The old man replied, 'I'm going to treat Red Plume who has returned home with an arrow in his side. He lives in that big tipi across the camp circle. As I get near, I call out, "To doctor I come, rattle and horn." When the people hear that, they all go indoors so that I may treat Red Plume without any curious onlookers.'

"Hakela asked, 'What medicine do you use?' After the medicine man showed him, Hakela tied him up and touched him with the coup stick to count first coup. Then taking the bundle on his own back he turned toward the village and started calling out, 'To doctor I come, rattle and horn.' The people all went into their tipis so Hakela went on to Red Plume's tipi. The relatives there all welcomed Hakela, anxious that he treat Red Plume and remove the arrow. Hakela had tried to disguise himself as an old man, but Iktomi the trickster known as Spiderman, who had invited himself to stay with Red Plume, kept saying, 'This is not the medicine man.' The relatives were all afraid that he would anger the old man and sent Iktomi away.

"When Hakela had carefully removed the lucky arrow, he placed it to one side and then he asked Red Plume if he could stay overnight. He explained that it was late and he was old and tired. The relatives made a bed of furs for him and they all settled down for the night. Luckily Red Plume seemed to be all right after the arrow was removed. When everyone was asleep, Hakela took the arrow and crawled out of the tipi. Iktomi was waiting outside. He began calling out and awakening everybody. 'This is not the medicine man. This is not the medicine man.' So they all began to chase Hakela. But Hakela was wearing his turtle shell moccasins and the riders on their fastest horses could not catch him. Hakela reached home and placed his brother's lucky arrow back where it had been hanging. He also hung the coup stick, feeling sad because he would not be able to tell anyone he had counted his 'first coup' on the medicine man, and he placed the strike-a-light bag back near Third Brother's backrest.

"His brothers did not reach home until very late that night. Hakela did not tell them of the scarlet bird or of his adventure. And he vowed never to use any of his brother's lucky belongings again."

Chano sighed, "I wish I had turtle shell moccasins like Hakela." Tasinagi laughed. "You have many lucky things and people. Look at your beautiful mother and do you remember the time you killed your first buffalo?" Chano replied, "Wakan-tanka has blessed me in many ways, but the best blessings are you, Father, Ate and Mother, Ina."

The Wicked Sister-in-Law

For many moons Tahcawin had been working on a new tipi, for the old one was worn from much use and travel. At last the tipi was finished and placed in the camp circle.

When Chano saw his new home, he was very excited. It was beautiful—large and painted on the outside. As he en-

66

tered the lodge, he decided that it was even more beautiful inside. The painting on the dew cloth, or inner lining, that made a wall hanging completely around the inside of the tipi was in geometric designs of clear colors. Parfleches, or containers made of rawhide, also painted in bright colors, were placed beside the backrests for his mother, Tah-cawin, for his father, Tasinagi, and for himself. He knew that his mother had carefully packed the parfleche containers with their personal belongings. It was his responsibility to be sure that his own things were always in the correct place in case they needed to move on quickly and unexpectedly. He hoped they would stay here a long time. Since winter was coming on, perhaps they would.

The beds were covered with soft thick furs. The little fire in the center pit burned brightly, spreading a welcome warmth. He sat down carefully on his bed of furs and smiled happily at his father and mother. They all looked about them silently. At last Tasinagi said to Tahcawin, "Lila waste. Very good!"

On the skin hanging was a picture record of Chano's grandfather and one of his father, a story of an important event in their lives.

Chano thought to himself that never had he seen a more interesting dew cloth. He had been well trained to relate the story of his people. He knew that for many, many years his father and his grandfather and his great-grandfather and those before him had been leaders among his tribe. The stories on the dew cloth were not new to him. But suddenly for the first time he realized that because of this beautiful skin hanging completely around the inside of the tipi, the lodge was warm.

"Ate," Chano said to his father, "whoever thought of the dew cloth was very clever. It has two uses: one to keep us warm and one to make our lodge more beautiful."

Tasinagi laughed and replied, "Yes, my son, but one time the dew cloth answered still another need for a very evil woman." Chano stretched out on the soft furs and begged, "A story? Oh, please tell me of the evil one and how she used the dew cloth."

Tasinagi smiled, "A story, yes, and about a very beautiful but evil woman."

"A long time ago one of the great hereditary chiefs of our tribe realized that he had become too old to be an active leader. He was blessed with two handsome sons. The older son, White Feather, was a natural leader, strong and brave. The younger son, Brave Bear, was his brother's closest companion. They were the best of friends.

"The old chief and the head men of the tribe gave a feast and dance and proclaimed White Feather the new chief. The whole tribe, including Brave Bear, his brother, was very happy.

"The women of the tribe made a large tipi for the two young brothers. When White Feather and Brave Bear moved into it, they were delighted to find that it was beautifully decorated. The dew cloth around the interior had pictures of White Feather's success in battle, with Brave Bear fighting right beside him.

"The tipi was in the inner circle close by the one in which White Feather and Brave Bear's father, mother, and sister lived. It was good. The sons talked and debated decisions with their wise old father.

"One day a band of visitors arrived in the camp. Among them was the daughter of one of the head men. Her name was Winona, meaning first born and she was very beautiful. When White Feather saw her, he decided she would be his wife. He brought many horses and gifts to her father's tipi. Soon after, he brought the beautiful girl home as his wife. When Brave Bear began to take his belongings back to his father's place, Winona protested. 'Always,' she said, 'you two have been close companions. Now I am your sister and you are part of our family.'

"Brave Bear was overjoyed to stay with them. He admired his new sister not only because of her beauty but because she was skilled in all the arts of Lakota women. Their clothing and everything else was made with greater skill than any other woman in the tribe possessed. Everyone admired her.

"As the months went by, Winona found that the people of the tribe loved and respected her husband as a great leader. He was always calm, dignified, and just in his decisions. But Winona also discovered that his brother, Brave Bear, was beloved by all because of his wonderful sense of humor and his joy in living. He drew everyone to him with his gaiety. People came to him with their troubles. They would talk with him more frankly than with his brother. Brave Bear in turn would always counsel them saying 'My brother and I . . .' Always the two were together and Winona began to feel very jealous of their relationship.

"Because of her great beauty and the fact that she was their firstborn, her parents had always given her all she wanted. She expected to be always first in the thoughts of her husband. She was jealous of Brave Bear because she realized that he was more handsome than her husband, but she also found that in spite of herself she enjoyed his laughter and fun just as much as the other people. Slowly she began to hate Brave Bear. He seemed always to be the center of attention when they were with others. She felt her husband no longer noticed her as he had when they were first man and wife.

"Slowly throughout the summer months she began to think of a plan. At first she tried to interest Brave Bear in some of the young girls in the tribe, hoping he would marry one of them. Then as she realized how close the two brothers were, she decided to destroy Brave Bear in some way. She tried to charm and attract Brave Bear by her great beauty, but he remained as gentle, as kind, and as brotherly to her as before.

"She began to take long walks every day. She always went to the pine grove and sat there imagining all the accidents that could easily be arranged for her brother-in-law.

"One day she noticed a badger watching her. To her great surprise he spoke to her and she could understand him. He told her how beautiful she was; he did not like to see her look so sad. Badger said, 'You are as beautiful as the wild roses here on the prairie. If I could find a gift worthy of you, I would bring it you. I wish only to watch you when you come to the pine forest. To be with you here is my whole life and happiness.'

"Winona was delighted to find someone who was

charmed by her great beauty. She spoke often with the badger and told him of her jealousy. Badger loved her so much he asked only that he be allowed to help her in any way that would make her happy again.

"It was the month of Changing Colors. The two brothers often went on hunting trips together and sometimes separately with groups of other friends.

"One day Brave Bear and some friends left early on a hunting trip, hoping to be back by the midafternoon. While he was gone, White Feather and some of the head men of the tribe were summoned to visit with another band about a half day's ride away from the camp. The Chief did not expect to return until late in the evening.

"After he left, Winona suddenly decided to put her plan into final action. She left the camp as though going on one of her long daily walks to the pine grove. When she reached the forest, she found her badger friend waiting. She prayed Badger to do her one favor. When he consented, she concealed him under her robe and returned home.

"In the tipi she had removed the furs from her brother-in-law's bed. She had moved all the belongings stored between the outside and the dew cloth to make a free space completely around the inside. She placed the door flap in a manner to indicate she was not to be disturbed.

"She showed Badger the space under her brother-in-law's bed. She asked him to dig out a deep hole as quickly as possible. Badger obeyed the wicked woman. As he dug, she collected the earth on several small skins and packed it around the tipi in back of the dew cloth where it was completely concealed from the inside and outside. Winona and the badger worked quickly and quietly.

"She took another stroll away from the village when they were about halfway through their task. When she was sure some of the people had seen her, she returned to the tipi. She found that Badger had dug a deep, deep pit, just the size she had indicated.

"Winona was very tired, but with the badger's help she managed to conceal all the earth behind the dew cloth. She thanked Badger for helping her and led him out of camp.

"Returning to the tipi, she quickly put everything back in place. She covered over the deep hole with furs so well that it looked exactly like his bed.

"Winona made a great effort to be seen going about her duties in the afternoon. As soon as she heard the shouts of the returning hunters, she took her usual place in the tipi.

"Brave Bear did not return at once. She knew he was taking care of storing the meat he had butchered and watering his horses and turning them loose.

"When Brave Bear entered at last, she greeted him graciously. He was tired and immediately threw himself down upon his bed. Down, down he fell into the pit. He was so surprised, he did not call out. The furs did not help break the fall very well as he hit his head sharply on the large rock Winona had placed at the top end of the pit. As he lost consciousness, she tossed down old dirty pieces of skin hoping to smother him.

"Quickly she replaced the bed and covered it with all the best furs she had. The tipi appeared as it had always been.

"Shortly after, White Feather returned, calling the men to gather in council. He announced the tribe would have to prepare to move camp as soon as possible. The band they had just visited had been harassed by groups of Crow Indians intent on stealing horses. He sent for his brother, but Winona told the messenger that Brave Bear had taken a side of meat to an old man who lived alone a good distance from the main camp.

"After a search that failed to find Brave Bear, the tribe began to believe that he had been captured by the Crow. There was great sadness, for if this was so, Brave Bear was now dead.

"The family was brokenhearted. They cut their long hair, they slashed their arms, they denied themselves food, and mourned the death of their son and brother. The whole tribe mourned Brave Bear.

"It was an ancient custom for the Lakota people to move away from the place where a person had died. So the people moved quickly to a more safely situated camping spot miles away. It was also the custom to leave behind the tipi and the dead person's belongings just as he or she had left them. Winona took only her own and her husband's personal belongings. She made sure the tipi was left almost as it had always been. She even left food for Brave Bear's spirit to feast upon. She took charge of the family's move while apparently mourning Brave Bear's death. Actually she was congratulating herself on the timing of the sudden move that helped conceal her horrible deed. Because she had withdrawn into the companionship of the two brothers in the last two months before Brave Bear disappeared, she now had no close friends. She kept to herself, busy with many wifely duties. She was no longer jealous. White Feather missed his brother very much and became closer to his wife than he had ever been before. She began to use her beauty and influence in many ways that were not always good for the people of the tribe.

"Soon after the band had moved on to their new home, the old camping ground was overrun by hungry wolves, coyotes, and birds eating everything they could find.

"An old wolf, still hungry, began to chew on an end of the buffalo robe on Brave Bear's bed. To his surprise he heard a human voice calling weakly for help from below the furs. He commanded several of the young wolves to pull the furs away. When at last they saw the young man lying in the pit, they were amazed. The old wolf now ordered four of the strongest wolves to help this human up out of the pit; they were not to attack or molest the young man in any way. Brave Bear was so weak from his ordeal in the pit that the old wolf decided he must be carried to their den in the mountains.

"The wolves spread one of the buffalo robes from the bed on the ground and placed the man in the center. Then many of the strong young wolves took the edges of the robe in their teeth and started off homeward to the hills. They were followed by the old wolf and his brothers and the coyotes and foxes. The wise old wolf commanded his brothers to carry all of the man's belongings: his parfleche cases, his arrows and bow, anything they felt he would want when he was able to move about again. The young man realized that he was a prisoner of these wild animals and in all probability his end would be a horrible death.

"He prayed to Wakan-tanka for help. He decided to

trust his animal brothers and show no fear.

"When they reached the den among the rocks, he was taken to the Wolf Chief, who was very wise and very old. The young man was allowed to open one of the parfleche cases, and after eating some of the wasna, or pemmican, that had been packed in it and drinking some water, he felt much stronger.

"Wolf Chief showed the young man a great many coyotes, foxes, and wolves who were crippled, blind, or disabled. These poor animals had been caught in traps set by men and had been rescued by their animal brothers.

"Wolf Chief said, 'My brother, you were rescued from a trap. You have escaped death because of us. We ask you to live among us and destroy traps laid for us and hunt large game for us to feed to these poor animals. If you will do this for us, we will live in peace and friendship.'

"Brave Bear thanked the Wolf Chief for saving his life and pledged himself to be a real brother to his animal companions. Wolf Chief sent word to all his animal brothers to respect the young man and protect him from harm.

"When Brave Bear was strong again, he went on a hunting trip with the wolves. He found a small herd of buffalo grazing near a stream. He ordered his companions to remain quiet as he crawled through the bushes. When he was

close enough, he shot the buffalo closest to him. The rest of the herd stampeded over the hillside.

"Brave Bear skinned and butchered the buffalo, cutting it into small pieces so each wolf could carry the meat easily in his jaws. On their way back to the den Brave Bear saw an elk in the woods. He was quick enough with his bow and arrow to kill the elk. He repeated the process of butchering and carving the meat into small pieces. By that time other foxes, coyotes, and wolves joined in carrying the meat back home. There was great rejoicing among all the animals.

"Wolf Chief was well pleased. He asked the animals to wait until the young man had prepared his own meal. He ordered a fire to be made at once. The little red foxes brought more than enough firewood and stacked it in the center of the rocky enclosure.

"Brave Bear roasted some of the buffalo meat over the fire. After he had finished eating, he carefully banked the fire, for he planned to hunt for the right stones with which to start his own fires again.

"Wolf Chief asked Brave Bear to lie down and cover himself completely with the blanket. He said, 'Your friends will be devouring the buffalo and elk. While they eat, I warn you not to uncover your face. Often the animals toss discarded bones into the air, so do not look on.'

"The young man did as he was instructed. He heard a terrible commotion, roaring and growling. At last Brave Bear was so curious he decided to lift a corner of the blanket to see what was going on. Just as he peered out, a sliver of bone flew into one of his eyes. Wolf Chief ordered the feast stopped at once. He knew what had happened to Brave Bear. He announced that a bit of bone had lodged in one of the man's eyes and would have to be removed. Now a bird called Magpie hopped up to the man and sat upon his nose. Carefully with his beak he picked the bone out of his eye. Brave Bear thanked Magpie and then his animal friends resumed their feast.

"Brave Bear roamed over the hills and plains and through the forests always accompanied by foxes, coyotes, and wolves. He loved playing with the little foxes. He had no fear of his animal brothers.

"On one of these trips they came to a big camp. Carefully Brave Bear destroyed the traps laid for the animals. As quickly as he did so, the little foxes helped themselves to the bait. When young boys from the camp came the next morning to inspect their traps, they were puzzled to find them all destroyed and the bait gone.

"Brave Bear lived with the animals a long time. But every time he came upon one of the large camps, he looked to see if they might not be his relatives. He wished that he might see his parents and his brother and sister again. But he still felt very bitter toward his sister-in-law.

"Wolf Chief was very old but very wise. He was also very fond of the young man and realized that he longed to return to his people. He spoke to Brave Bear of a plan. At first Brave Bear refused to believe that Winona would in any way harm or influence White Feather. But Wolf Chief told him that an evil person could hurt people in secret ways just as Winona had tried to destroy Brave Bear, and so Brave Bear at last decided to accept the plan of Wolf Chief. Although his people often accepted the murderer as a member of the family of one he had killed, Brave Bear did not feel able to accept his sister-in-law and give her the punishment of living with his family while he was alive.

"At last he made his farewells to all of his animal friends and after he gave a last farewell look at Wolf Chief, he was escorted by hundreds of wolves, foxes, and coyotes over a long distance to the camp of his people. When they arrived at the camp, it was dark. The animals stayed back in the hills and let him find his way down to the tipis.

"Brave Bear made his way to the first tipi, which was very small and insignificant. He peered in and was astonished to see his own father and mother and sister there.

"Quietly and without saying a word, he slipped into the tipi and sat down beside them. He was dismayed to see their poor and sparse belongings and all the indications that they still mourned him. Or did they mourn for their other son? Finally his sister glanced at him. She then whispered to her mother, 'Mother, look there, it is my brother who has returned.' But the mother did not raise her eyes to look and replied, 'No, it is one of his friends.'

"Brave Bear said in a loud voice, 'Ina, Mother, Ate, Father, I have come back to you.'

"His father, mother, and sister were overjoyed. They threw their arms about him and when they found him a living being, wept for joy.

"At last his father ran out to the center of camp and announced that his lost son had returned. The whole camp turned out to greet him and give him many gifts. In his honor they gave a great feast. He told them the story of living with the wild beasts in the hills until he was able to return to them.

"White Feather, his brother, stood by his side, delighted and happy, while Winona also stood beside them, coldly beautiful and quiet. After the feast that night Brave Bear returned to the lodge of his parents.

"The next day White Feather asked Brave Bear to walk

with him and tell him of his adventures. He asked Brave
Bear why he had not returned to his tipi that night, as it had
always been his home.

"Brave Bear told his brother the true story of the accident. He also told him of his understanding with the wise
old Wolf Chief. Because of Winona's crime she was to be
sent in his place to be the captive of the animals.

"White Feather thought long and seriously about the
story. He realized how happy Winona had been since Brave
Bear was gone, how often she had persuaded him to make
decisions against his better judgment. More and more he
realized how she had forced his parents to live as they had
since his brother disappeared. He folded his buffalo robe
around him closely and sorrowfully replied, 'Yes, Brother,
my wife shall be delivered to the beasts of the forest and
hills for what she has done to you.'

"The next day the Chief gave an order for the tribe to go
on a buffalo hunt. As the party prepared to go out, Brave
Bear asked his sister-in-law to accompany them. The guilty
woman was anxious to please him in any way and consented
to join them. She did not take part in the chase when they
found the buffalo herd but joined them when they were
skinning and butchering their kill. When the other people
left for home, they stayed on a little longer.

"At the time Wolf Chief had planned, Brave Bear turned toward the hills and called, 'Here is my sister-in-law. Come and take her now.'

"At that signal hundreds of wolves, foxes, and coyotes charged toward them from every direction. Brave Bear and White Feather lost sight of Winona as the animals led her back to the hills.

"Silently the two brothers began their mourning for a beautiful but evil woman."

Chano rolled over on his fur bed and felt the solid earth beneath. He looked at his father and said, "It is such a sad story."

Tasinagi smiled and replied, "Not all sisters-in-law are evil. Do not judge people by one bad person. Evil deeds are often punished in very strange ways and at unexpected times. Be happy that we live among good people."

He laughed as Chano reached over and peeked under the dew cloth. "No earth there," Tasinagi said. "But as it gets colder we will pack the space with dry grass to help insulate the tipi from the cold. Think now only of the beauty of our lodge and the goodness of your mother."

Chano sighed, then smiled lovingly at his mother and father.

Iktomi and
the Red-Eyed Ducks

Chano loved the long winter evenings of the Month of
Frosted Tipis. Then his mother would do her quill work
and his father would tell his stories about Iktomi, the Spiderman or Trickster. Iktomi was always playing tricks on
people or animals or birds and always something happened

to Iktomi instead. Chano would stretch out on his bed of buffalo robes. It was always warm in the tipi. The small fire in the center burned brightly and cast its strange shadows on the tipi walls and the dew cloth.

"Please, Ate, tell me a story about Iktomi," Chano would plead.

"Which one do you wish to hear this evening, my son?" his father would ask.

"This time the one about Iktomi and the red-eyed ducks," answered Chano.

Tasinagi began the old familiar tale and even Tahcawin chuckled in joyful anticipation.

"One day Iktomi the Spiderman went for a walk along the river. A little way down the river he saw a flock of ducks floating near the shore. 'Oh, ho,' said Iktomi, 'they're so fat and I'm so hungry for roast duck.' He sat down on a log and he started to think. He scratched his head on one side and then on the other because he knew this would help him think of a way to catch the ducks. At last he took off his blanket and put it on the ground. He filled it with dried grass and then he rolled it up into a bundle. Iktomi put the bundle on his back and began to run. As he came near the ducks, they watched him. They were surprised to

see the Spiderman running with a bundle on his back. Iktomi was generally a very lazy being.

" 'Ho, Little Brother, why are you running so fast?' called out the ducks.

" 'Because the Lakota-oyate are having a feast and a dance. They want me to sing for them. There are songs in the bundle on my back,' answered Iktomi.

" 'Oh, ho, he has songs,' said the ducks in wonder. They had never heard of anyone carrying songs in a bundle. 'Will you sing for us? We would like to dance, too.'

" 'Oh, I haven't time, I'm in a great hurry,' replied Iktomi.

" 'Please don't go yet. Sing for us just a little while. And let us see the songs in the bundle,' called out the ducks.

" 'Very well, but you must hurry. And I can't let you *see* the songs. But I can sing them for you. Come and stand around me in a circle.'

"When the ducks had formed a circle around him, Iktomi said, 'I will stand in the middle and sing. But you must all close your eyes while you are dancing. I cannot let anyone see my songs. And if you open your eyes, your eyes will turn red.'

"All the ducks promised not to look. They shut their eyes and they began to dance around Spiderman. And as they danced, he sang and beat on his drum. 'Alas for him who looks, his eyes will turn red.' As they danced by Iktomi, he would pick out the fattest duck and knock him over the head with his drumstick. Of course that made an odd sound. It didn't sound like the regular beating on the drum. Every once in a while there would be a dull thud.

"One of the little ducks grew very curious about this sound. At last she opened one eye just to look a little. And at that point Iktomi was just putting a nice fat duck onto his blanket. At once the little duck screamed, 'Look ye, look ye, Iktomi is killing us.' At this cry all the remaining ducks opened their eyes and flew away. And as Iktomi looked up at them, he began to laugh. His power had worked; sometimes he wasn't so lucky and it backfired. Every single one of those ducks had red eyes and so they have to this very day."

Chano laughed and begged for the rest of the story. But as it was late, Tasinagi said, "Tomorrow I will tell you how Iktomi lost his roast duck dinner. Go to sleep now and dream of good roast duck to eat."

The next night Chano stretched out on his fur bed again. He looked expectantly at his father. Tasinagi, teasing, said, "Chano, you know the rest of the story about Iktomi and the ducks." Chano only smiled because he knew his father would tell it to him as many times as he wanted. It was one of his father's favorite stories about Iktomi too.

"Iktomi pulled the blanket with the dead ducks in it over toward the woods that were close to the river. He was busy for a while gathering firewood and starting two different kinds of fires. First he dug a small pit, lined it with stones, and built a fire on them. Then he built a fire a little way from the pit in the shade of the trees and arranged a spit over a fire. He plucked a few ducks for the spit and arranged them in such a manner that they would cook rather quickly. The other ducks he put in the pit and covered over with earth and stones so that they would cook slowly. He was happy that he had thought of this way. After he had finished his first duck dinner, he would rest until he was hungry again; then the ducks in the pit would be ready to eat.

"All this activity had tired Iktomi, so he stretched out under the shade of the trees and tried to sleep. But just as he closed his eyes, he heard a scraping sound, a very annoying sound. He looked up at the trees above him and saw that the wind was making two branches scrape against each other. The sound continued and Iktomi could not sleep. He decided to climb up and separate the two branches. Up he went and just as he put his hand between the branches, the wind stopped blowing. There he was with his hand caught so tightly between the branches he could not get loose. Just then Iktomi from his perch up in the tree saw a fox trotting along down by the river. Iktomi muttered to himself, 'Fox, Fox, do not come this way. Stay away from my ducks.' But Fox could not help but smell the roasting ducks and hear the sizzling of the fat as it fell into the fire below the spit. He ran over, and knocking off one duck, began to eat greedily. Poor Iktomi tried to get his hand loose so that he could get down and protect his dinner, but he could not. He was so angry he began to scold Fox, 'I caught those ducks and they belong to me.'

"Fox looked up in amazement. When he saw Iktomi stuck in the tree, he just laughed and went right on eating heartily. Poor Iktomi's mouth watered at every savory bite Fox took. He begged him to leave one duck for him, but Fox just laughed at him again. When he had finished the last duck, he started to trot off. Iktomi was so angry by this time he called out, 'I hope you ate too much. But at least you did not find the others.'

"Fox stopped in his tracks and thought this over. He decided to come back for a last look around. There were no more ducks on the spit. Iktomi began to weep and wail. Fox sniffed around the ground. Before long he found the pit. Fox dug all the ducks up and placed them on Iktomi's blanket. Taking one end in his mouth he began to run along the side of the river toward his lair. He was full of duck, but he had friends who would enjoy eating duck as much as he did.

"Just when Iktomi lost sight of Fox, the wind began to blow again. As soon as the branches parted, Iktomi pulled his hand away and slid down the tree. He rushed over to the spit; no ducks. He looked in the pit, feeling around in case Fox had missed just one small duck; no ducks. Poor Iktomi could not stand smelling the delicious odor of roast duck so off he ran in the opposite direction to spend the night dreaming about the dinner that he did not have."

Chano stretched out on his fur bed and began to laugh. And then he looked at his father and said, "Wouldn't it be nice to have a roast duck dinner tonight?"

Tahcawin laughed too. She said, "You had nice buffalo ribs for dinner tonight. Remember that and dream about them."

The Lakota Woman

Chano snuggled down in the warmth of his fur bed. Before his mother had gone off to visit in one of the nearby tipis, he had greeted his father's guests. He was a bit uneasy because a number of his father's friends and some of the old men of the tribe were talking about one of their friends who had recently died. Chano tried to reassure himself by thinking, *but we are all men and men are brave.* But Chano did not feel very brave.

He watched the small fire in the center of the tipi. As the men sat around it, their shadows were projected grotesquely on the dew cloth inside. Some of the men wondered whether or not the dead could return to earth as Wanagi, or ghosts. Some said no; others were sure they could and told of various experiences to prove their point. Finally Grandfather was asked his opinion.

"Why should you doubt?" White Weasel asked. "Does not the Great Mystery say that we shall live again? And as for a Wanagi appearing on this earth, I myself have seen it."

There was an immediate request for the story and of course Chano was all ears.

"It was the year after that of the many Crow wars," began Grandfather. "Our people had been victorious, but there were many tipis where the dead and the missing were still mourned. I was one of a hunting party that left camp in search of game. But luck was not with us and after seeking for over a week and finding nothing, we decided to separate and travel in different directions, meeting the third day at High Peak. Then he who had located the game country would lead the others back to it.

"It was the Month of Dry Grass, the Moon of Scarlet Plums, and though the days were warm and comfortable, the nights called for a fire and a warm robe to sleep in. I found a good place for a camp just as the sun was setting and decided to stay there for the night. There was plenty of dry wood for a fire, grass for my horse, and water not too far away. The place really was very fine, but my horse did not seem to like it. He kept pawing the ground and looking about him and snorting as if in fear. Though he quieted down when I approached him and stroked his head, he began his odd actions again the moment I left his side. Thinking that he might have scented some wild animal, for I knew there was no enemy around, I tethered him close to me and built a fire big enough to last all night. Then I prepared to sleep.

"Though I was tired and knew I should rest, sleep would not come to me. My robe was a warm one and yet from time to time I shivered as if from cold. Looking toward my horse, I could see he too was shivering. Thinking that the Old Man from the North was paying us a visit, I put still more wood on the fire and then lying down once more I closed my eyes. I may have slept. I know not. But I do know that suddenly I heard a groan, a groan of unutterable anguish, and then a terrible gurgling sound, then a silence. Was I dreaming? Before I could decide, the air about me was filled with the cries of many men, war cries, battle cries, the sound of guns. I jumped to my feet. Too late. I was surrounded by the enemy and I knew that all that was left for me was to die as a brave man should. My horse was still near me but reeling and neighing and trying his best to break loose. I grasped my gun and pointing at the enemy nearest me, fired. At the sound there was a flash and a blood-curdling cry. And my horse with a supreme effort broke the line he was tied with and went galloping off into the night. As the sound of his feet grew fainter and fainter, I looked about me and saw that I was alone. No warriors, no enemy in sight, nothing. But the fire had been extinguished as if some gigantic hand had just snuffed it out.

"I must be asleep and still dreaming. And then almost at my very side I heard again that terrible groan, followed by that equally horrible gurgling sound. I am not a coward. I have faced the enemy when he far outnumbered me, but that enemy I could see. But this–again that groan. Not waiting even to pick up my robe, I started racing in the direction my horse had taken. Fear lent me wings. Fear gave me strength. I ran and ran until the first rays of the dawn appeared in the eastern sky.

"But as fast as I ran and as far as I went, I could hear the sound of steps pursuing me. By good fortune I found my horse. The rope about his head had caught in some bushes and held him fast. I mounted, and still shivering with fear, started in the direction of High Peak where I knew the rest of the party would be waiting for me. All day I traveled and all day I heard those footsteps behind me. Finally I summoned all my courage and looked around. There some hundred feet behind me was a woman. A woman of my own band. A woman who I recalled had been among the missing after one of the battles with the Crow. I stopped. I turned toward her and she vanished into the air.

"My horse, now beyond my control from fear, started galloping with me and never slackened his pace until we were in sight of High Peak. The others were already there and much to my surprise asked me why I did not bring the woman who was following me into the camp. I looked to where they pointed and there she stood. She never moved. She gave no sound. Just stood there watching . . . watching. It was then I told them what had happened. They laughed and would not believe me.

"One of them started toward her to head her into camp and again she vanished. Fear broke out among us and it was then that Great Eagle, who was wise in many ways, spoke. 'You have no cause for fear,' said he. 'Had it been an

evil spirit, our brother here would have never reached us. Rather has this Wanagi come to ask our aid or perhaps to render aid to us. Come, let us follow where she leads. We are not children, we are men.'

"And as if in answer to his words the figure appeared once more and this time when we approached did not vanish but glided on before us. We followed and in the afternoon we came upon the spot where I had camped. The figure continued on until she reached a clump of trees, where she vanished. To the trees we went too. There was nothing. But wait, there was something. A tinkling sound as of dry sticks hitting against each other. It seemed to come from overhead. And peering up into the thick branches we saw something swaying, swinging back and forth as it swayed. It gave forth the sound that we had heard. We climbed up the tree and brought it down. It was the body of a woman—no, just a skeleton—and wrapped around it was the dress of the woman who had followed me, the woman we had followed in turn, the woman who had led us to the place where she had died. We wrapped her in a robe and gave her burial. And with her burial came peace. The horses no longer showed fear. And as if in reward for what we had done, we discovered the country around was filled with game.

"Years later I heard the story of her death. When the enemy attacked, she climbed the tree and hid among the leaves. All would have been well except the branch on which she rested broke. She fell and in some way a rope that she had with her coiled around her throat; the other end catching in the fork of the branch held her there until she choked to death. The enemy would have cut her down and saved her life, but just then her own people rushed upon the scene and drove them off. And so there she stayed until her restless soul compelled us to give her bones the rest that all should have. Yes, this was one time that the dead did return."

Just as his Grandfather finished the story, Chano felt a quiet movement beside him. A gentle hand smoothed his hair back from his face and he knew his mother was there. He had not heard her come into the tipi.

With her beside him Chano felt so safe and secure he soon fell asleep. That night he did not dream of Wanagi as he had expected. He had decided that the Wanagi were not to be feared.

Tonweya and the Eagles

Everyone was excited. It was the Month of Grass Appearing, and the whole camp was busy getting ready to move over the plains to a new home. They would be close to more game and they looked forward to the move. Everyone that is except Chano. He loved this camping spot and already felt lonely for the distant hills.

Tahcawin had packed the parfleche cases with clothing and food and strapped them to a travois made of two trailing poles with a skin net stretched between them. Another travois lay on the ground ready for the new tipi.

Chano was very happy when Tasinagi suggested the three of them ride up to their favorite hills for the last time.

As the three of them rode along, Tasinagi called Chano's attention to the two large birds circling overhead. They were Waŋbli, the eagle. Chano knew they were sacred to his people and that they must never be killed.

He looked at the eagle feather in his father's hair, a sign of bravery, and wondered why it was that the Lakotas as well as many other Indians held Waŋbli, the eagle, in such great respect. Someday he would ask his father about this.

The two eagles they were watching did not seem afraid of the three travelers. They flew nearer and nearer, swooping down in ever narrowing circles. They seemed to be trying to attract the attention of the travelers.

Suddenly Chano called out, "Look, Ate! The feathers on their wings are tipped with red. I never knew that Waŋbli had red feathers!"

"Are you sure of this, my son?" Tasinagi asked.

"Yes, Father. Both birds had tips of bright red on their wings."

"Tahcawin," said Tasinagi, "our son has been favored by the sight of the sacred birds of Tonweya. Few have seen them and it is a sign of good for him."

"What do you mean, Ate?" asked Chano. "What are the sacred birds of Tonweya?"

"They are the eagles who saved Tonweya's life many, many snows ago. Tonweya was a great chief and a great medicine man."

Chano immediately begged his father to tell him the story. Tasinagi motioned for Chano to ride by his side and began:

"It was the summer when the big ball of fire fell from the sky. A band of Lakotas were camping just about where we are now. Among them was a young man whose name was Tonweya. He was not only good to look upon, but he was a great runner and hunter. He was very brave in the face of danger. Everyone said that someday he would be a chief. Brave and good chiefs are always needed in every tribe.

"One day Tonweya went out hunting. He found a small herd of buffalo grazing near the hills and picking out a young fat cow sent an arrow straight into her heart. While he was skinning the buffalo, he noticed a large eagle circling above him. Watching her flight he saw that she settled on a ledge of rock projecting from a high, steep cliff about a quarter mile away. Tonweya knew there must be a nest there. He was determined to find it. If there were young eaglets, he could capture them and raise them for their feathers.

"He looked carefully at the ledge. He saw it would be impossible to climb up to it from the plain below. The only way was from above and getting down would be very dangerous. After skinning the buffalo, Tonweya cut the green hide into one long narrow strip. Then he stretched and twisted the strip through the dust until he had a long strong rope of hide.

"Coiling this about him, he made his way to the tip of the cliff right above the eagle's nest on the ledge. Fastening one end of this rawhide rope to a jack pine, he let the other fall over the ledge. Looking down he saw that it hung within a few feet of the nest. His plan was to slide down the rope and tie the eaglets to the end. Then after he had pulled himself up again, he could draw them up after him. Great honor would come to him. A pair of captive eagles would supply feathers for many warriors.

"Tonweya carefully lowered himself over the edge of the

cliff and soon stood on the ledge. There were two beautiful young eaglets in the nest, full feathered, though not yet able to fly. He tied them to his rope and prepared to climb up. But just as he placed his weight on the rope, to his great surprise it fell down beside him. The green hide had been slipping at the knot where he had tied it to the tree; when he pulled on it to go up again, the knot came loose and down came the rope.

"Tonweya realized immediately that he was trapped. Only Wakan-tanka, the Great Mystery, could save him from a slow death by starvation and thirst. He looked below him. There was a sheer drop of many hundreds of feet with not even the slightest projection by which he might climb down. When he tried to climb up, he could find neither handhold nor foothold. Waŋbli had chosen well the place for a nest.

"Despite his brave heart terror gripped Tonweya. He stood looking off in the direction he knew his people to be. He cried out, 'Ma hiyopo! Ma hiyopo! Help me!' but only the echo of his own voice answered.

"As the sun was setting, the mother eagle returned to her nest. She screamed in rage when she saw a man with her eaglets. Round and round she flew. Now and then she

106

would charge with lightning speed toward Tonweya and the young birds. The two eaglets flapped their wings wildly and called out to her. Finally in despair the mother eagle made one more swoop toward her nest, and then screaming defiantly, flew off and disappeared. Night fell and the stars came out. Tonweya was alone on the ledge with the two little birds.

"When the sun came up, Tonweya was very tired. He had not slept during the night. The ledge was so narrow, he was afraid he might roll off if he fell asleep. The sun rose high in the heavens and then started its descent into the west. Soon it would be night. Tonweya looked forward with dread to the lonely vigil he must again keep. He was very hungry and so terribly thirsty.

"The second day Tonweya noticed a small spruce growing in a cleft of the rocks some four feet above him. He tied a piece of his rope to this tree and he fastened the other end around his waist. That way even if he stumbled, he would not fall off the ledge. More important still, he could chance some sleep, which he needed badly.

"The third day passed as the others had; heat, hunger, unquenchable thirst. The hope that some of his people might come in search of him was gone. Even if they came, they would never think of looking for him on the cliffs. The mother of the eaglets did not return. Tonweya's presence had frightened her away.

"By this time the two eaglets, seeing that Tonweya had no intention of hurting them, had made friends with him. They allowed Tonweya to touch them at will. Tonweya could see that they were as hungry as he was, so taking out his knife he cut small pieces from the rawhide rope and fed them. This act of kindness removed the last vestige of fear they might have had. They played all about him. They allowed him to hold them aloft. They flapped their wings bravely as he lifted them toward the sun. As he felt the upward pull of their wings, there came to him an idea. Since he had no wings of his own, why could he not make use of the wings of his eagle brothers? He raised his arms toward the sky and called upon Wakan-tanka for wisdom.

"The night of the third day, the one on which he had fed the eaglets for the first time, was raw and chill. When Tonweya stretched out for what little sleep he could get, he shivered with the cold. As if understanding his need, the two little eaglets left their nest and coming over to where he lay nestled their warm, fluffy bodies close beside him. In a few moments Tonweya was asleep.

"While he was asleep, he dreamed. In his dream Wakan-tanka spoke to him. He told him to be brave, the two eaglets would save him. Tonweya awoke suddenly. The eagles were still beside him. As they felt him move, they nestled even closer to him. He placed his arms around them. He knew that his time to die had not yet come. He would once more see his people. He was no longer afraid.

"For days thereafter Tonweya fed the rawhide rope to his eagle friends. Luckily it was a long rope, for it was, of course, almost a whole buffalo hide. But while the eaglets thrived on it and grew larger and stronger each day, Tonweya grew thinner and weaker. It rained one day and water gathered in the hollows of the rocks on the ledge. Still he was very hungry and thirsty. He tried to think only of caring for the eaglets.

"Each day Tonweya would hold them up by their legs and let them try their wings. Each day the pull on his arms grew stronger. Soon it was so powerful it almost lifted him from his feet. He knew the time was coming for him to put his idea into action. He decided he must do it quickly, for weak as he was he would be unable to do it after a few more days.

"The last of the rawhide was gone, the last bit of water

on the ledge was drunk. Tonweya was so weak, he could hardly stand. With an effort he dragged himself upright and called his eagle brothers to him. Standing on the edge of the ledge he called to Wakan-tanka for help. He grasped the eaglets' legs in each hand and closing his eyes he jumped.

"For a moment he felt himself falling, falling. Then he felt the pull on his arms. Opening his eyes he saw that the two eagles were flying easily. They seemed to be supporting his weight with little effort. In a moment they had reached the ground. Tonweya lay there too exhausted, too weak to move. The eagles remained by his side guarding him.

"After resting awhile Tonweya slowly made his way to a little stream nearby. He drank deeply of its cool water. A few berries were growing on the bushes there. He ate them ravenously. Strengthened by even this little food and water, he started off in the direction of the camp. His progress was slow, for he was compelled to rest many times. Always the eaglets remained by his side guarding him.

"On the way he passed the spot where he had killed the buffalo. The coyotes and vultures had left nothing but bones. However his bow and arrows were just where he had left them. He managed to kill a rabbit upon which he and his eagle friends feasted. Late in the afternoon he reached the camp, only to find that his people had moved on. It was late. He was very tired so he decided to stay there that night. He soon fell asleep, the two eagles pressing close beside him all night.

"The sun was high in the sky when Tonweya awoke. The long sleep had given him back much strength. After once more giving thanks to Wakan-tanka for his safety he set out after his people. For two days he followed their trail. He lived on the roots and berries he found along the way and what little game he could shoot. He shared everything with his eagle brothers, who followed him. Sometimes they flew overhead, sometimes they walked behind him, and now and then they rested on his shoulders.

"Well along in the afternoon of the second day he caught up with the band. At first they were frightened when they saw him. Then they welcomed him with joy.

"They were astonished at his story. The two eagles who never left Tonweya amazed them. They were glad that they had always been kind to Waŋbli and had never killed them.

"The time came when the eagles were able to hunt food for themselves and though everyone expected them to fly

112

away, they did not. True, they would leave with the dawn on hunting forays, but when the evening drew near, they would fly back fearlessly and enter Tonweya's tipi, where they passed the night. Everyone marveled at the sight.

"But eagles, like men, should be free. Tonweya, who by now understood their language, told them they could go. They were to enjoy the life the Great Mystery, Wakan-tanka, had planned for them. At first they refused. But when Tonweya said if he ever needed their help he would call for them, they consented.

"The tribe gave a great feast in their honor. In gratitude for all they had done Tonweya painted the tips of their wings a bright red to denote courage and bravery. He took them up on a high mountain. He held them once more toward the sky and bidding them good-bye released them. Spreading their wings they soared away. Tonweya watched them until they disappeared in the eye of the sun.

"Many snows have passed and Tonweya has long been dead. But now and then the eagles with the red-tipped wings are still seen. There are always two of them and they never show any fear of people. Some say they are the original sacred eagles of Tonweya, for the Waŋbli lives for many snows. Some think they are the children of the sacred ones. It is said whoever sees the red-tipped wings of the eagles is sure of their protection as long as he is fearless and brave. And only the fearless and brave may wear the eagle feather tipped with red."

When Tasinagi finished the story, he looked to see if the red-winged eagles were still following them. They were there. He knew then that his son Chano was one of those to be blessed by great good in his life.

Epilogue

When Chano grew up and had children of his own, he often recalled the stories he was told during the days of his boyhood. And when the old men came to visit him, they would tell him about the battles in which they had fought, about the Sun Dances and the ceremonies in which they had taken part.

Listening to these stories so vividly told was an unforgettable experience for us. We are three daughters: Rosebud, the eldest; Chauncina, named for my father; and Evelyn.

When Chano was in Canada among the Ojibway, he was delighted to hear their old stories. When he came to New York City, he found many new friends among those who were world travelers and they too had stories to tell. He was not surprised to find that many of the old stories were very much alike.

He told his daughters, "People all over the world have their own way of life, but through their stories we find that we can understand them and live with them. Do not isolate yourselves, you will learn from others."

As Badger Clark, the poet laureate of South Dakota, said of him: "Having known two worlds Yellow Robe is good for any third."

Glossary
and Pronunciation Guide

Ate (ah-*tay*) father

Canowicakte (chah-*no*-way-chahk-tay) kill-in-the-woods

Coup (koo) to strike or to hit

Hakela (hah-*kah*-lah) last born

Iktomi (ick-*tow*-me) Spiderman or Trickster

Ina (ee-*nah*) mother

Keya (*kay*-yah) turtle

Lakota-oyate (lah-*coat*-tah o-*yah-tay*) many tribes in
   one nation

Lila waste (*lee*-lah wash-*tay*) very good

Mato (*mah*-tow) bear

Ma hiyopo (*mah* he-yo-po) a call for help

Mitawa (me-*tah*-wah) very dear

Parfleche (*par*-flesh) a rawhide container

Tahcawin (*tahk*-sha-weeah) fawn

Tasinagi (*tah*-she-nah-ghee) yellow robe

Tonweya (tone-*way*-ya) guide

Waditaka (*wah*-dee-*tah*-kah) brave

Wakan-tanka (wah-*kahn*-Tahn-kah) the Great Mystery

Waŋbli (wahm-*blee*) eagle

Wanagi (wah-*nah*-ghee) ghost

Waziya (wah-*zee*-yah) god of the storm

Wasna (wahz-*nah*) a pemmican, a type of dried food

Wastewin (wash-*tay*-weeah) good

Wayuwaka (*wah*-yoo-*wah*-kah) peacemaker

Winona (*we*-no-nah) first born

Rosebud Yellow Robe, a descendant of Sitting Bull, is a well-known storyteller. She has held many workshops in libraries and public schools, bringing her listeners an authentic picture of Indian life long ago. In 1989 the W. H. Over State Museum and the Institute of Indian Studies held a Rosebud Yellow Robe Day at the University of South Dakota. They honored her for "a lifetime commitment in communicating the values of her people to non-Indians and serving as a powerful model for Native Americans who sought ways to preserve their culture."

Rosebud Yellow Robe was born in Rapid City, South Dakota, and now lives in New York City.

Jerry Pinkney is a two-time Caldecott Honor Book winner—once for *The Talking Eggs* (Dial) by Robert San Souci. He is the only artist to have been given the Coretta Scott King Award three times. *The Patchwork Quilt* not only won the Coretta Scott King Award, but also the Christopher Award, and was an ALA Notable Book and Reading Rainbow selection. Mr. Pinkney is Associate Professor of Art at the University of Delaware and Visiting Professor in the Department of Art at the University at Buffalo. He lives with his wife, Gloria, in Croton-on-Hudson, New York.